THIS BOOK BELONGS TO

MARTY

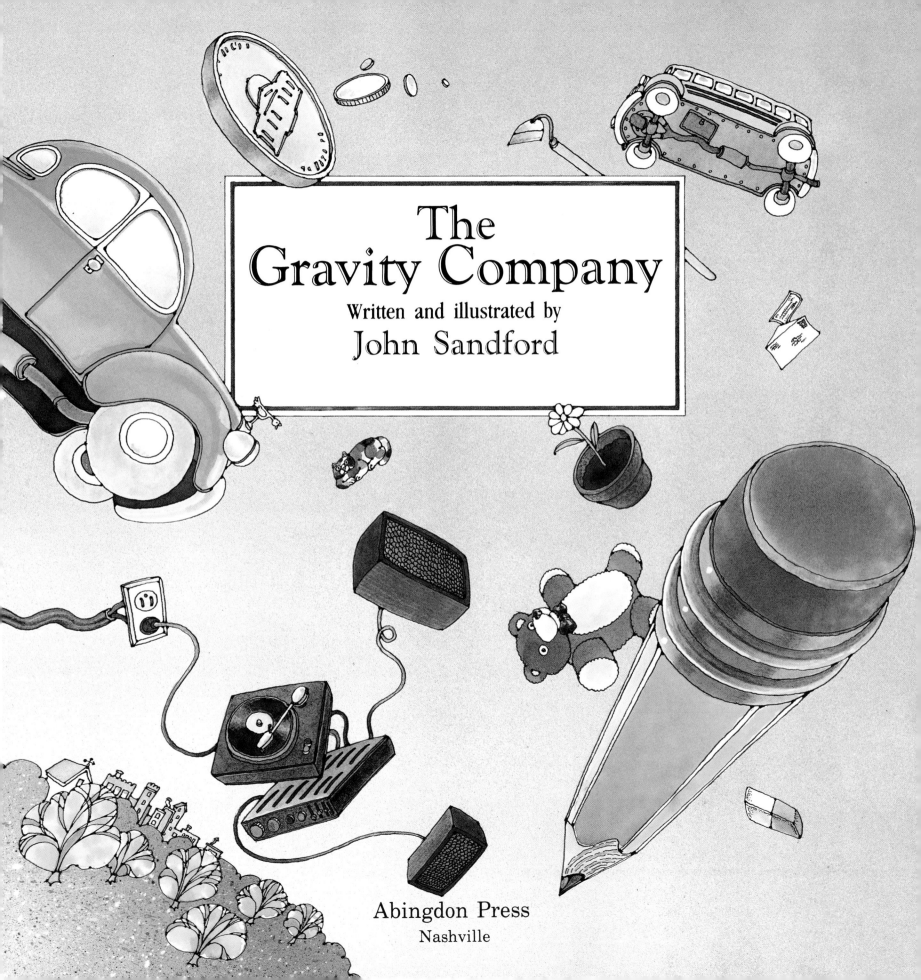

The Gravity Company

Written and illustrated by
John Sandford

Abingdon Press

Nashville

For
Frances,
my center
of
gravity
     js

Library of Congress Cataloging-in-Publication Data
Sandford, John, 1944–
  The Gravity Company.
  The summary: Extraordinary things happen in
Cayuga Ridge, a small quiet town where everything
runs correctly, the day the switch at the gravity
company is accidentally turned off.
  [1. Gravity—Fiction]   I. Title.
PZ7.S2165Gr 1988   [E]   88-10549
      ISBN 0-687-15686-6 (alk. paper)

Printed in Singapore

Cayuga Ridge has always been a small, quiet town.

On the main street are the Cayuga Ridge Laundry, the Cayuga Ridge Bakery, the Cayuga Ridge Pizza Parlor, the Cayuga Ridge Telephone Company, the Cayuga Ridge Library, the Cayuga Ridge Courthouse with the statues of Cayuga Ridge heroes, and the Cayuga Ridge Gravity Company.

At the Gravity Company, Mortimer makes sure the machine always works. Mortimer watches the dials and gauges. Mortimer pulls the levers, throws the switches, and pushes the buttons. It is Mortimer's job to see that the people of Cayuga Ridge always have enough gravity.

Mortimer makes sure the Gravity Company runs well.

Every day at noon, Mortimer switches the Gravity machine to *automatic*. He puts on his rubber boots, his jacket, and a hat. Mortimer always grabs an umbrella, just in case it rains. Every day at noon, Mortimer goes next door to have lunch.

Every day at noon while Mortimer is next door having lunch, Gloria, the cleaning woman, enters the Gravity Company. Every day at noon, Gloria brings in her mops and buckets, brooms and brushes, rags and soap to clean the Gravity Company.

A Gravity Company runs well when it is clean.

One day at noon, while Mortimer was next door having lunch and Gloria was using her mops and buckets, brooms and brushes, rags and soap to clean the Gravity Company, something happened.

The handle of Gloria's mop hit the *automatic* switch on the Gravity machine.

A Gravity Company does not run very well when the gravity has been turned off.

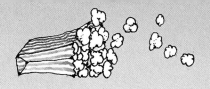

All over Cayuga Ridge things began to
happen. Without gravity, nothing had weight.
Without gravity, there was nothing to keep
things from floating away.

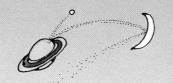

At the Cayuga Ridge Park, the baseball game had to be stopped. Ham Sam had knocked the ball into outer space. Ham Sam did not smile very often, but he smiled at that.

At the ranch on the edge of town, Cowboy Hiram was riding Crazy Daisy, the wildest bronc around. Crazy Daisy kicked Cowboy Hiram into the clouds.

Now that there was no gravity, Cowboy Hiram could ride a cloud. He liked riding a cloud better than riding Crazy Daisy.